Badger
the
Mystical Mutt
and the Enchanting Exchange

McNicol & Jackson

JF

THE LUNICORN PRESS
Glasgow
Text © Lyn McNicol and Laura Cameron Jackson 2013
Illustrations © Laura Cameron Jackson 2013
All rights reserved

First published 2013 by The Lunicorn Press
1

Printed by Martins the Printers, Berwick-upon-Tweed
Designed and typeset by Heather Macpherson at
Raspberry Creative Type
Set in 14.25 pt Gentium Book

British Library Cataloguing in Publication Data
A CIP catalogue record for this book is available from the British
Library

ISBN: 978-0-9569640-5-2

www.badgerthemysticalmutt.com
www.facebook.com/badgermutt
www.twitter.com/badgermutt

For Myra McNicol

A round of "up-paws" for
Badger the Mystical Mutt

"Pitch-perfect subtlety and wit."
Shari Low, The Daily Record

"Using Badger books is an excellent way of opening communication channels with how your child gets on at school."
Missing Sleep

"There are some underlying morality themes that should allow vigorous class discussions."
Stephen King, The School Librarian Magazine

"I don't know how McNicol and Jackson do it but they have a prodigious talent when it comes to Badger the Mystical Mutt - they are fun, have wickedly good illustrations and a plot line to keep both children and adults happy."
BFK Books

"Kids' book takes world by storm."
The Scottish Sun

"A moving and joyful story which warmed the heart of this cynical old journalist."
That's Books

"First-time winner."
The Evening Times

Chapter One

It was three thunderclaps from lightning, and all was eerily still on the lane. In Badger's garden, where the Mystical Mutt had been practising his latest, spectacular "bowls of toast" trick, nothing moved.

Badger sniffed the air above. "Any moment now," he said nervously.

Suddenly, the sky lit up with a dazzling blast of lightning, followed almost immediately by another flash. Badger counted the seconds between the flashes, then heard the familiar rumble and roll, boom and crack of the storm.

"Time to take cover before the clouds burst," thought Badger, frowning at the gloominess above. "Nippy Nimbus must be really cross up there."

He quickly gathered up his coloured bowls and his sparkly tablecloth, and ran to shelter in his shed.

Further along the lane, Pogo Paws and Pickle, the new joint leaders of the gang, were having a blazing row. A travelling circus had arrived in town and Pickle was *not* happy.

"I don't care if you *did* spend all your puppy years in the circus. We're not going, and that's that!" snapped Pickle.

"But a circus has never visited here since mine left that day," whined Pogo Paws. "It could be *my* circus, and if it is ... I could see my family again."

"Well, if it's the same circus, and the same family, that left you behind to fend for yourself all those years ago, *why* would you want to go back there?" she sneered.

Just then, another bolt of lightning

flashed over the lane, followed by an almighty roar of thunder.

"Quick! The storm is nearly here," shouted Pogo Paws, grabbing Pickle's paw. "Over there. We can hide in the bins."

"Don't be silly," said Pickle. "That's dangerous. Some of the bins are shiny. We could be struck by lightning. No, let's go to Badger's shed instead."

As Pogo Paws and Pickle ran towards Badger's garden, the first heavy thuds of rain fell on the lane. They sprackled clumsily through the crack in the fence and knocked on the door of Badger's shed.

"Hurry up! Come on in," said Badger, ushering the dripping pair out of the downpour, which was now pelting off the roof.

Pogo Paws and Pickle shook themselves and peered through the window at the torrent of rain outside.

Pogo Paws shivered. "Thank goodness we're in here, and not out there."

"Surely this means the circus can't go ahead," said Pickle hopefully. "The grass will be too squelchy after the rain."

Pogo Paws whimpered.

"Why are you so sad, Pogo Paws?" asked Badger gently. "If it doesn't go ahead tomorrow, there will be other circuses, and other times. Although, I've got a guest spot on the magic stage, so I really want it to go ahead too."

As Pogo Paws opened his mouth to speak, Pickle interrupted. "He wants to see if it's the circus he came from, and if any of his old pals are still there."

"It's not just old pals, Pickle. It's my *family*," muttered Pogo Paws.

"You're from a travelling circus, Pogo Paws? I had no idea," said Badger excitedly.

Pogo Paws' tail started to wag slightly. Pickle scoffed "Here we go ...".

The little dog puffed out his chest and said proudly, "Yes, I was their star acrobat. That's where I got my name and how I learned to bounce so high. I loved it."

"So why did you leave?" asked Badger.

"I didn't," sighed Pogo Paws. "I got left behind by mistake when the circus moved on. It was my own fault really, as I was exploring this very lane. I ran and ran to catch up, but couldn't find them, and that's how I ended up here ... with *her!*" He nodded his head at Pickle wearily.

Pickle scowled.

As the rain continued, puddles grew into bigger puddles, and weeds sprang up from the muddy grass. It was 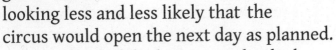 looking less and less likely that the circus would open the next day as planned.

At the end of the lane, near the duck pond, the candy striped tents of the circus sagged. The flags, which had been all aflutter earlier, now hung limply. The sawdust was sodden and the trailers were caked in mud. Everything was wet and washed-out.

"We'll just have to wait and see," said Badger hopefully. "In the meantime, I know what will cheer us all up. I can show you my trick for tomorrow night's show. I'm still a bit rusty, but it's almost there."

Pogo Paws and Pickle both groaned.

Badger assembled his assorted dinner bowls and stood back. He crossed his paws

backwards and forwards, to and fro, up and down, tapped each bowl with gusto and started the spell.

"*One two tickety boo, turn these bowls into ...*"
He stopped and scratched his head.
What's wrong?" asked Pogo Paws.

"I can't quite remember the rest of the rhyme."

Suddenly, the bowls began to vibrate, as hundreds of slices of toast burst out in all directions. The buttery toast swirled and birled around their heads, filling the shed. Pogo Paws, Pickle and Badger slipped and slid, and they all ended up flat on their backs.

"I think you've got a bit more work to do on that one," shouted Pogo Paws, over the crunch and the crumble of the countless crusts.

Badger smiled sheepishly. "Er, yes. If I could just remember the spell ..."

Backstage at the circus Big Top, in a sturdy cage, behind iron bars, flanked by two vicious guard dogs, there came a roar bigger than any thunderclap.

The huge beast grunted and lay down in the corner of the cage.

On a lamp post at the other end of the lane, a poster advertising the circus announced:

Introducing ...
*the only living Minotaur in **this** world!*
Fresh from the mysterious land of Esterious,
our star attraction is half-big-folk, half-bull.
Come and see it ... if you dare!

Chapter Two

The next day dawned with a blazing sun. Badger emerged from his shed, sniffed the air and smiled. A moment later, Pickle appeared too, blinking in the brightness of the sunshine.

"It looks like the circus will go ahead after all," said Badger.

"Do we really *have* to go?" groaned Pickle.

The shed burst open as Pogo Paws bounced into the brand new morning.

"Woweeeeeeeeeeeeeeee! What a brilliant day! We can go to the circus today. Hooraaaaaaaaaaaaaaay!"

Pogo Paws bounded round Badger's garden with glee.

Pickle looked at Badger sulkily, and said: "I don't want to go to the circus. It's all *he* ever talks about. So what if he's homesick? I'm fed up with it."

"Oh, Pickle, look at how happy he is. Surely you can turn that frown upside-down and go along with Pogo Paws. It's only for one day. Besides which, I've got my star turn there later this afternoon. Come for me ... please?" Badger pleaded.

Pickle sighed. "Okay, I suppose, if I really must."

"Right then, you two, off you go back to the lane, I've got some serious practising to do before tonight's show," said Badger.

As Pickle and Pogo Paws headed for the crack in the fence, Badger was already setting out his coloured bowls and trying again to remember the spell.

Backstage, at the circus, the minotaur felt its eyes sting with tears, as the ringmaster jangled keys outside its cage.

"Not long now, Beast!" bellowed the moustached ringmaster. "Then you can run free inside the ring, to amaze and astound the crowds."

The minotaur sighed.

"Look a bit more fierce! You're our star attraction. Get up ... now!" ordered the ringmaster, cracking his whip.

The minotaur ducked and pawed the ground with its chunky boots. Through gritted teeth, it let out an almighty roar.

"That's more like it. That's what keeps our audience terrified. Keep it up!"

Outside the tent, the sideshows and fairground were in full swing. Music blared, lights shimmered, candyfloss billowed and coconuts shied.

Pogo Paws and Pickle arrived at the circus.

"Right, Pogo Paws, you have to win me something for coming here today," announced Pickle.

"Of course. Take your pick. Which stall do you fancy?" replied Pogo Paws, with a swagger.

Pickle looked at the stalls and thought for a moment.

"I could do with a collar actually. I've never had one before, so if you could win me one of them, then I *might* start to enjoy myself today," said Pickle.

"That, my dear, should be easy-peasy

lemon squeezy. Let's head over
to that stall there," pointed
Pogo Paws.

In front of them
stood a hexagonal
booth jam-packed
with every shape,
every size and every
colour of dog and
cat collar. In the
middle hung three
circular hoops,
with a sign that
said: "*Try your
luck at scoop the
hoop. Three crunchy-
munchy chewy chops
for three shots. Throw the
ball through the hoop to scoop a prize!*"

Pogo Paws handed over three of his
treasured crunchy-munchy chewy chops,
and picked up the brightly coloured balls.

"Stand back, Pickle. Watch and learn!"
said Pogo Paws confidently.

He eyed the hoop and took aim. His first ball bounced off and fell to the ground. Pickle smirked. "Not so easy after all, Pogo Paws!"

Pogo Paws frowned and took aim with his second ball. It too bounced off the hoop and missed.

"Hang on a minute!" shouted Pogo Paws. "The balls are too big for the hole in the hoops. It's a scam. Watch this, Pickle. I'll get that collar for you."

With his third and last ball, Pogo Paws bounced and bounced until he was level with the hoop. He flew forward and squeezed the foam ball neatly through the hoop.

"There, I won. I'd like my prize now, please," said Pogo Paws proudly.

The stallholder scowled and grumbled: "You cheated!"

"No, I didn't" said Pogo Paws indignantly. "*You* cheated! And if you don't give me my prize, I'll tell the others on the lane and then no one will visit this stall."

The stallholder grimaced, waved his arm across the prizes and told him to choose what he wanted.

Pogo Paws asked Pickle to pick her collar.

Pickle's eyes widened in delight. She took her time looking at them all, and then selected a lilac satin collar with pink lovehearts.

"Let me!" said Pogo Paws, as he fastened the new collar gently around her neck.

Pickle smiled adoringly at her hero.

"*Now* I'm enjoying myself. Thank you so much, Pogo Paws, for winning me this. Okay, let's go and see Badger's show."

As Pogo Paws and Pickle took their seats in the audience, the spotlight shone in the centre of the circus ring. The air was thick with anticipation.

Suddenly, the ringmaster swept into the ring with a flourish, and announced: "And now, for your delectation and delight, be

24

prepared to be badgical-magicalled with your very own local 'Wizard of Paws'. I give you ... Badger the Mystical Mutt!"

The crowd roared as Badger strutted into the spotlight, his coat swishing and his eyes sparkling.

He turned around and wagged his tail at his audience, which erupted with thunderous applause. Badger smiled and shook his paws. In front of him was a table with a sparkly red-and-white spotted tablecloth. On top of the table lay three coloured bowls: a red-spotted one on the left; a stripy yellow one in the middle; and a swirly blue one on the right.

Badger stood back with his head held high. He lifted each bowl and showed the audience that there was nothing underneath, then crossed his paws over the bowls. Sparkles of light swirled around him, and he uttered the spell:

"One two, tickety boo, three four, toast galore ..."

The bowls rumbled noisily on the table, and as Badger lifted the red-spotted one, he revealed a slice of hot, buttered toast. The audience gasped.

He lifted the stripy yellow bowl, and there, in front of him, were two slices of toast. The audience gasped again.

Badger winked, took a bow and pointed at the third blue bowl.

Just as he was about to lift the bowl to show the *three* slices of toast beneath,

and await his final applause, there was an almighty roar and a pounding of chunky boots from behind.

The ground shuddered as a huge beast rumbled past, upturning Badger's table and his precious magic trick.

The audience screamed as the creature lunged towards them, and ran off in all directions, rushing to escape the mayhem and chaos. But amid all the ruckus, the ringmaster was nowhere to be seen.

Badger watched in horror as the circus tent emptied in a frenzy. Then he saw the horns of the star attraction — the minotaur — disappear from the ring.

Chapter Three

Later that night, Badger trudged back to his garden, his box of tricks filled with the coloured bowls and cold toast.

Already, "Wanted!" posters were pinned to lamp posts and tree trunks all over the lane and beyond, for the escaped circus act.

"My moment in the spotlight was stolen by an escaped minotaur. I can't believe it!" muttered Badger.

Just then, there was a rustle at the end of the garden. Badger looked up and saw two horns peeping over the top of the fence. As he moved closer, he heard a sobbing snort.

"Hello?" he shouted. "Who's there?"

"Are you Badger the Mystical Mutt?" replied a gruff voice from the other side of the fence.

"Yes, I am indeed. How can I help you?" asked Badger warily.

The horns moved higher to reveal the head of a bull.

Badger gasped. It was the escaped minotaur from the circus.

"I want to go home," snivelled the beast. "I'm fed up of performing every night!"

"Where is home?" asked Badger gently.

"My lovely labyrinth in Esterious, but it's not in this universe."

"Aha! That could be a bit tricky with travel then," said Badger smiling.

"Yes, but I've heard you've got a Wim-Wim which goes to the Enchanted Forest. And *I* believe there's a unicorn there who can help me," said the minotaur hopefully.

"Yes, that might be correct. But the Wim-Wim wouldn't be able to take you. You're too big; you're enormous!"

"But I heard there might be a portal for Esterious somewhere in a cave there," wailed the minotaur.

The minotaur cried again.

"It's okay" said Badger softly. "Maybe we could try one of my special shrinking spells, to make you fit into the Wim-Wim."

The beast looked at Badger sadly. "I've

heard about your spells too, Badger. But they don't always work, do they?"

Badger twitched and rubbed his white tuft at the top of his head: "That may be so, but my magic in the circus worked okay, until *you* stole my limelight by escaping."

"Sorry about that," said the minotaur. "But can you still help me?"

"I'll try my best. What's your name anyway?"

"Minty."

"Minty the minotaur. I like it. Right then, Minty, let me think of my shrinking spell, because we need to get you off the lane as soon as possible. There are 'Wanted!' notices everywhere. You're a runaway, and probably dangerous."

"I'm not dangerous. I'm a big softie really. It's only the ringmaster who makes me roar," said Minty meekly. "I don't suppose there's any chance you could magic me up some alfalfa hay, could you? It's my favourite and I'm starving." The minotaur smiled endearingly at Badger.

The Mystical Mutt shook his head. "First things first, Minty," he said. "We need to make you smaller, not bigger after a feast of hay."

The minotaur crouched down as Badger consulted his big book of spells under '*How to hide a minotaur*'.

"Ah!" said Badger triumphantly. "Found it! So, let's try this for starters:
With saffron rice and all things nice,
Hocus pocus, and focus on the crocus ..."

As Pogo Paws and Pickle walked homewards from the circus towards the lane, Pogo Paws was down in the dumps.

"Okay, so it wasn't *your* old circus! So what?" muttered Pickle, thoughtlessly.

"But it's made me feel worse. I'm even more homesick now. I miss my family," shrugged Pogo Paws.

"Whatever!" sighed Pickle, and then she spotted the 'Wanted!' posters.

"Look, there's a reward!" said Pickle excitedly "If we could find the minotaur, we could get a year's supply of crunchy-munchy chewy chops. Woohooooooooooooo!"

"Isn't getting a brand-new collar enough

excitement for one day, Pickle?" asked Pogo Paws wearily.

"Uh oh! What's *that* I see outside Badger's garden," yelled Pickle. "Look, there it is! It's the minotaur talking to Badger. Quick!"

Pickle sped towards the crack in the fence at Badger's, but there was nothing to be seen. The minotaur had vanished.

Pickle stopped suddenly. "I'm sure I saw it," she said, mystified. She peeked behind the wheelie bins, and then into Badger's garden, but all she could see was Badger holding a bunch of crocuses.

"Did you see a big beast with two horns and chunky boots a moment ago?" Pickle shouted to Badger.

"Er ... no. Not round here. I think I would have noticed that," fibbed the Mystical Mutt.

"Come on, Pickle," urged Pogo Paws. "It's late and I need to go to bed. Let's just leave it tonight."

Pickle sighed, and grumbling about disappearing minotaurs, she followed

Pogo Paws further up the lane to their
box, a little miffed, but still with her collar
displayed proudly. However, as they lay
down to sleep, Pickle could not forget
the vision of the escaped minotaur, and
decided to alert the circus ringmaster first
thing in the morning.

Back in Badger's garden, an invisible
minotaur was exasperated.

"Sorry!" said Badger sheepishly "That went a bit skew-whiff. I got my invisible spell mixed up with my shrinking spell. Don't worry, I'll fix it. Where are you exactly?"

Minty groaned and shook his invisible head.

Chapter Four

The next morning, Pogo Paws awoke with a long yawn and a stretch. He rubbed his eyes and turned around to speak to Pickle, but there was an empty space where she usually lay.

I wonder where she's gone, thought Pogo Paws, peering up and down the lane. *She's normally a sleepy head in the morning.*

While Pogo Paws gave himself a good scratch and pondered on his pal's whereabouts, Pickle was already at the circus tent talking to the ringmaster.

"I saw it. I definitely saw it up the lane, outside Badger the Mystical Mutt's garden," said Pickle urgently.

"Are you sure? It's really big with two horns, chunky boots and a cape," said the ringmaster doubtfully.

"I'm three million times sure. The minotaur was right here in the lane. And I'll bet Badger the Mystical Mutt has something to do with it," she blustered.

"Okay then, but we've searched the lane. However, I'll round up the clowns again, and send them in."

"Follow me," said Pickle. "Then, when I'm proved right, do I get my reward?"

"If what you say is true, then you can have your reward gladly," said the ringmaster.

Yum yum, thought Pickle.

In Badger's garden, the Mystical Mutt was still trying to make Minty visible when Pogo Paws arrived in a fluster.

"Have you seen Pickle this morning, Badger?" asked Pogo Paws anxiously.

"Not since last night, when she thought she'd seen the minotaur. Speaking of which, I have a rather urgent spell to do right now. So, if you'll excuse me?" Badger turned his back on Pogo Paws and said:

"Right, Minty, concentrate. Here goes:
With saffron rice, sugary mice,
And a droplet of some honeydew,
Reverse, unwind, twist and find,
And bring my friend here into view."

Badger stepped backwards and turned around three times to face where he thought Minty was. Sparkles of light appeared around him, and suddenly he was knee-high to the minotaur. Pogo Paws gasped.

"It worked, it worked!" yelled Badger happily.

"Uh oh!" said Minty, pointing to a row of bright red noses lining the top of the fence behind Badger.

Badger turned around to see the clowns' hooters and Pickle peering through.

"Told you he was there!" she shouted gleefully. Pogo Paws closed his eyes in despair.

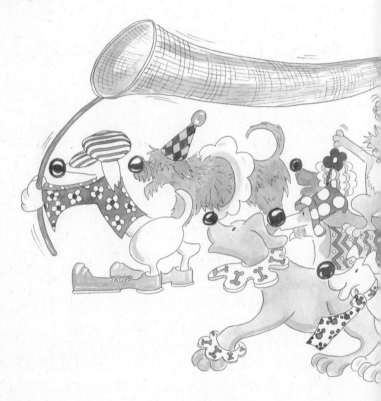

Suddenly, six clowns, one ringmaster, three acrobatic cats and a ten-legged Cockerpoo rampaged through Badger's garden with a huge net, and attempted to throw it over the minotaur, who was trembling next to the sundial.

But Badger was ready with his next plan.

"Show koo ray, show koo ray,
Make these intruders go away,
'Chief, chief, do your stuff,
Make the minotaur tough enough.
Let him soar in the sky above,
And glide along like a peaceful dove."

Badger's red neckerchief unfurled immediately from his neck, transforming itself into a sturdy helicopter propeller. It attached itself to Minty's backbone, and soon the enormous beast was hovering in the air.

The clowns flapped their feet, the ringmaster bellowed and swiped, the acrobatic cats leapt and the Cockerpoo yelped, but no one could catch Minty.

The ringmaster huddled with his crew and then emerged with a stack of Minty's favourite snack: delicious alfalfa hay.

"It's a sucker for this hay. This should do the trick. Stand back and watch!"

"Oh, Minty," shouted the ringmaster affectionately, fluttering his eyelashes and smiling sweetly. "Look what I've got?" He waved the hay above him, just under the minotaur's nose.

Badger put his paws over his eyes. He couldn't bear to look, as he'd already discovered how much minotaurs loved hay.

"Let me down, 'Chief'," pleaded the minotaur as he reached to sniff the tasty hay.

'Chief hovered lower.

"It's the *good* stuff — alfalfa — isn't it?" the minotaur asked in disbelief. "I only usually get *that* when we've had a sell-out."

"But we *will* have a sell-out if you come back to us, Minty," pleaded the ringmaster. "And you can have this every day, because we *love* you."

'Chief sighed, stopped flapping and returned to Badger's neck, as Minty landed on the ground. The clowns surged forward and threw the huge net around the minotaur.

"Great! Now, you'll be in time for the next show. Back to work!" yelled the ringmaster, yanking the hay out of reach.

The minotaur, not quite sure how he'd actually managed to enter Badger's garden in the first place, followed his captors to the fence, his shoulders slumped.

"Oh, before I forget, here's your reward," cackled the ringmaster, throwing Pickle a measly few crunchy-munchy chewy chops.

Badger and Pogo Paws glared at Pickle as Minty bust his way through the fence towards the circus, leaving a minotaur-sized gaping hole.

"So it was *you* who betrayed us?" said Pogo Paws angrily.

"I didn't betray *you*," said Pickle defensively, "There was a reward for catching the minotaur, although *this is* hardly a year's supply," she added, looking scornfully at the couple of chewy chops in her paw.

"I am *so* disappointed, Pickle," frowned Pogo Paws. "How could you do that to Badger?"

Pickle shrugged.

"Pickle, the minotaur isn't happy in the circus. He desperately wants to go home, and came to me for help," said Badger gently.

"Well," said Pickle defiantly, "how on earth, was I supposed to know that?"

"You weren't," said Pogo Paws, "but now you do. I understand how it feels to be homesick, so we need to help the minotaur get back home. And in order to do that, we have to help it escape again. Are you up for it, Pickle?"

Pickle shimmied uncomfortably. "Is that allowed? After I've just picked up the reward for his capture?"

"Well, I won't tell if you won't," chuckled Badger.

But at the far end of the lane, posters were already appearing about the circus's forthcoming final performance.

The touring troupe was moving on at noon the next day.

Badger, Pogo Paws and Pickle didn't have long to form a plan to rescue Minty, and get him home to Esterious.

Chapter Five

Back in Badger's garden, the three dogs looked forlornly at the minotaur-shaped hole in the fence, and scratched their heads.

"If I could just perfect my shrinking spell, I could help the minotaur find his way home," said Badger.

"But we don't actually know where home *is* for him, apart from the fact it's in a labyrinth," said Pogo Paws.

"A *labby rinse?* Is that not where labradors have their baths?" asked a puzzled Pickle.

Badger sighed. "It's a *Labyrinth,* Pickle, and we're not likely to find one of them on the lane or anywhere nearby, because Minty said it was located in a parallel universe. Somewhere in Esterious, wherever that is!"

"A pally-well yooni verse? What's that then, rhyming friends?" asked an even more bewildered Pickle.

Badger smirked and explained: "A parallel universe, Pickle, is like another world that exists separately from ours ... but at the same time."

Pickle scratched her head.

They all sat and thought very, very hard.

Suddenly, Badger jumped up.

"I know who might be able to help me! Baby Unicorn! He knows about stuff like this. Plus," said Badger, trying to remember, "I'm sure Minty mentioned something about the Enchanted Forest and my unicorn."

"Ah!" said Pogo Paws. "Does this involve your famous Wim-Wim?"

"Indeed, it does, so I have to leave right now," said Badger.

"Can we come with you?" asked Pogo Paws and Pickle excitedly.

"Not this time, chums. You two need to go and see what's happening backstage at the circus. So scarper!"

Pogo Paws and Pickle left Badger's garden and headed for the circus.

When they arrived, there was hustle and bustle all around them. The performers were practising their act for the finale performance: jugglers juggled; acrobatic cats tumbled; clowns ruffled their collars and filled up their water squirters; baton-twirlers on stilts teetered; unicyclists raced; plate-spinners spun; trapeze artists swung; tightrope walkers balanced; and the rola-bolas see-sawed. As the brass band tuned up, a glockenspiel tinkled and the ringmaster, at the centre of it all, cracked his whip and twirled his handle-bar moustache.

Pogo Paws stood quietly watching it all. His heart ached to be part of it again, and to be back with his family.

"The smell of the greasepaint and the sawdust brings back so many memories, Pickle," said Pogo Paws, as a tear rolled down his face.

"Oh, pull yourself together!" said Pickle sharply. "This isn't the same circus *you* came from. You said it has never returned. It's probably in the same place as Minty's *labby rinse,* so get a grip. We've got work to do."

Pogo Paws sighed and muttered to himself. "I'd love to go home too."

Pickle ignored him, marched forward and shouted: "Follow me!"

They crept into the wooden benches for the audience, and crawled out of view on their tummies, towards the curtained stage entrance.

"Oh no!" said Pogo Paws. "They've got guard dogs at the backstage curtain. We'll never get past them."

"Right," said Pickle, "what we need is a disguise." Pogo Paws followed as Pickle crawled back to where the clowns were practising their slapstick routine. "Stay there," she whispered.

While Pogo Paws hid in the shadows, Pickle picked up a nearby juggler's ball and threw it as hard as she could. It landed just to the side of the clowns and rolled forward. Startled, the clowns stumbled towards the ball, leaving Pickle free to rush towards a trunk she'd spied. She dragged it back towards Pogo Paws.

"Let's see what we've got here." Pickle opened the lid of the clowns' dressing-up box.

"Wow!" said Pogo Paws, pulling out a multi-coloured spiky wig, a red nose, a bow tie and two huge flipper-shaped yellow shoes.

"Epic!" said Pickle, finding a wonky top hat with a squirty flower, a long fat neck tie, a harlequin jacket and a massive pair of spectacles.

"This should do the trick. Quick, put them on," instructed Pickle.

Meanwhile, in the Enchanted Forest, Badger had already arrived in the Crystal Cave and was explaining Minty's problem to his friend, Baby Unicorn.

"Badger, as Minty hinted, there's a portal right here for the labyrinth, but it only opens during a very rare total solar eclipse. The Big Folk call it a 'ring of fire'. But first, let me show you something," said Baby Unicorn.

The unicorn pointed its horn at the back wall of the cave, where a screen flickered into life. On it, Badger saw Pogo Paws as a pup, performing happily in a circus, and surrounded by his family. Then he saw Minty bumbling about his maze contentedly.

"So Pogo Paws really *did* come from a circus, and he really *is* homesick," said Badger. "But Minty is desperate to go home and I really want to help him."

Baby Unicorn sighed and said: "So, there has to be an Enchanting Exchange."

Badger stared at Baby Unicorn with his eyebrows twitching. He was well and truly flummoxed.

The unicorn continued: "An Enchanting Exchange is a bit like a Swap Shop. In order to get something you want, you have to give something away. Which means that for the minotaur to go back to his labyrinth, Pogo Paws must leave Pickle forever, and go back to his long-lost circus. Once the Exchange happens, it cannot be altered. It calls for some extremely powerful magic, as well as that all-important eclipse."

"But I can't *even* do a shrinking spell properly, never mind an Enchanting Exchange," said Badger apprehensively.

Back at the circus, Pogo Paws and Pickle could not stop giggling. They had now decided to call themselves "the Tumble Twins", and were enjoying their clown disguises. They walked straight through the stage curtains, undetected by the guard dogs.

Everything was in darkness. In a corner, they heard sobbing, and found the minotaur shackled inside his cage.

"Psssssssssssssssst! We're Badger's pals, Pogo Paws and Pickle. Look over here," whispered Pickle.

The minotaur lifted his head wearily and looked towards the whispered voice.

"You can't make me any more miserable than I already am. Hang on ... wasn't it you, Pickle, who told them where I was? And now I'm back here again."

"I'm really sorry," said Pickle, "But we're here to help you now. Look."

Pogo Paws and Pickle stepped closer till the minotaur could see them more clearly. Minty guffawed with laughter. "Really?

Dressed like that? What are you going to do? Boggle me with your buffoonery?"

"Badger is on the case. He's gone to see Baby Unicorn," whispered Pogo Paws. "So hang in there. We'll be back."

Minty shook his head in despair.

Back in the lane, Badger had returned to his garden. Time was running out.

I know exactly what I need, thought Badger.

At the back of his shed lay a pile of old spell books. He rummaged through them, and then spotted it: his book of *Potions, Planets and Plots*. He blew off the dust and carefully turned its ancient pages.

To his amazement, he discovered that there was a total solar eclipse scheduled for the very next day.

Chapter Six

Pogo Paws and Pickle scurried through the minotaur-shaped hole in Badger's fence. They were still dressed as the Tumble Twins, and startled the Mystical Mutt, who was busy working on his shrinking spell.

"It's us, it's us!" said Pickle excitedly. "Can't you tell? Gosh, these disguises really are awesome."

"Can you at least remove your snazzy spectacles and stop your flower from squirting water please, Pickle," said Badger, rubbing his eyes and shaking his head.

"Oops, sorry, of course!" grinned Pickle. "But we've had such fun, haven't we, Pogo Paws? I quite like being a clown."

"Good. Perhaps you can see now why Pogo Paws loved being in the circus."

Badger looked at Pickle pointedly. "Now, tell me, did you find Minty?"

"We did," said Pogo Paws proudly. "And we told him you were planning his escape. How did *you* get on with your pal, Baby Unicorn?"

"The portal for the labyrinth *is* in the Crystal Cave, and we can get Minty home. But it's not going to be easy. And there's one other tiny detail as well ..."

Pogo Paws and Pickle looked at Badger expectantly as he continued: "Pogo Paws must also return home."

Pogo Paws clapped his paws together, but Pickle looked confused.

"I don't understand, Badger. Pickle is already home ... here on the lane."

"Not really," said Badger softly. "This isn't your true home, is it, Pogo Paws? *Your* home is in the circus, where your family is too."

Pogo Paws nodded sadly and patted Pickle's paw. Pickle turned and ran off.

"You'll have to talk to her, Pogo Paws, because if you go back to your circus, it won't be easy to come back here to see

Pickle," said Badger seriously.

"I understand," said Pogo Paws. "I'll go and find her and explain."

As Pogo Paws turned to go after Pickle, he said, "Thank you, Badger. You've no idea how much this chance to go home means to me."

Badger nodded and walked over to his sundial to summon his Wim-Wim. He had another urgent trip to make. He had to get to the Ring of Brodgar to meet Captain Bravebark, for only *he* could tell him the spell required for the Enchanting Exchange.

Out in the lane, Pogo Paws searched high and low for his best friend, Pickle, but she was nowhere to be found. He sat down wearily in his box and looked fondly up and down the lane.

This had been his home for so long, since he'd been left behind by his beloved circus. He'd had great times here, and Pickle, although she scolded him constantly, had supported him through thick and thin. What if life wasn't better in the circus of his childhood, even though he would be back with his family? What if his life here on the lane, with Pickle, really was happier?

Under the shadow of the old oak tree, Pickle was hiding. She was crying. Pickle had never cried before, but she couldn't believe that her best friend, Pogo Paws, annoying as he was, was willing to abandon her forever.

Badger and his Wim-Wim had reached the Ring of Brodgar in record time, and Captain Bravebark was waiting to greet him.

"I got your p-mail, Badger. Everything is ready," shouted Bravebark. "Follow me."

Badger followed the Captain to a big, tall, sloping standing stone.

"Now, here is where we can ignite the spell, which will activate at exactly the right moment of the solar eclipse. Repeat after me:

With pebbles from Pluto,
And red dust from Mars,
Let the Enchanting Exchange
Begin with the stars ..."

Badger repeated the start of the spell solemnly, as Bravebark continued.

"With a solar eclipse
And a charmed bewitch,
Shine the light forth
     On this magical switch ..."

Badger repeated the end of the spell and stood back as a blast of light shone in the centre of the Ring of Brodgar standing stones.

"Wow!" said Badger. "Is that it? Is that all I have to do?"

There's a little bit more to it than that," the Captain

66

smiled. "But, most importantly, do you think you'll be able to remember the spell?"

"Of course," said Badger confidently.

"Now, you'll need Pogo Paws to be in the centre of the circus ring spotlight at exactly the same moment as Minty stands in the shaft of light at the back of the Crystal Cave. And that moment has to be exactly when the total solar eclipse occurs in the morning."

"Okay," said Badger nervously. "I'll need to take Minty to the Crystal Cave, which means I'll be relying on Pickle to take Pogo Paws to the circus. And right now, they're not even talking to each other. So, that bit could be tricky."

"Well, *you* have to make it happen. It's the only way it will work," said Captain Bravebark. "Now, you'd best get going, as time is running out. Let me know how it goes. Good luck, Badger."

Badger grinned anxiously, thanked his relative and stepped back into the Wim-Wim to begin his almighty task ahead.

But back at the old oak tree, Pickle was hatching a plan of her own to stop Pogo Paws from *ever* going home.

Chapter Seven

As Badger and his Wim-Wim drifted along the lane back to the garden, he could hear Pogo Paws shouting frantically over the clatter and clang of the engine.

"Badger, I can't find Pickle!"

"Oh no!" yelled the Mystical Mutt anxiously. "Without Pickle's help, the Exchange can't go ahead. We *need* to find her."

"But why Pickle, when it's me who's leaving?" asked Pogo Paws sadly.

"She has to help us shine the light, Pogo Paws, so we *have* to find her. Now, are you sure — very, very sure — you want to do this? Because once the Exchange has been made, you will be back in your original circus, and not here on the Lane," said Badger, landing the Wim-Wim with a wobble.

Paws nodded firmly. "Yes, I'm sure. I definitely want to be part of the Exchange with Minty. It's time for me to go back home to my circus. I miss my family."

While Badger told Pogo Paws all about his visit to Baby Unicorn and the Crystal Cave, and what needed to be done, Pickle had made her way to the candy striped tents and was sitting in the audience watching the final show at the circus. She knew that Badger only had that night to help Minty escape before the travelling show moved on the next day.

She was on alert for Badger's arrival, all set to ruin his plans.

But as Badger and Pogo Paws crept into the backstage area towards Minty's cage, they were totally invisible. Badger chuckled as he remembered how he'd got his spells mixed up before, when he was trying to help Minty.

"Good job I remembered my invisibility spell earlier, Pogo Paws. Otherwise, we'd never have got past those dogs on the door. Now, if I can just get my shrinking spell right this time, then we can get Minty out. But we'll need to wait until he's done his part of the show," said Badger.

"So, what do we do now?" asked Pogo Paws.

"We sit tight and wait. Or we could always join the audience and enjoy the show?" suggested Badger.

Pogo Paws pointed to the stage and Badger followed. They squeezed onto the end of a ringside bench and looked around the audience. It was packed. Suddenly, Pogo Paws spotted Pickle sitting with her paws folded, looking very cross.

"Look, Badger, there's Pickle. Gosh, I'm glad she's okay," said Pogo Paws, relieved.

Yes, me too," said Badger. "But I wonder why she's here, when she doesn't even like the circus."

All of a sudden, the brass band started playing and three floppy clowns rushed out clumsily, and paraded around the ring. Then, the ringmaster, in his splendid red hat and tails, emerged from the stage curtains.

"Good evening, everyone," he bellowed, twirling his moustache. "Are you ready to observe the greatest show on this earth?"

The audience cheered.

"Then sit back and get ready to be dazzled as I introduce to you our first act of the night. Spectacular aerial artistry from the blackest caves of Hairy Mill ... I give you ... the *Swing and Shout Sisters!*"

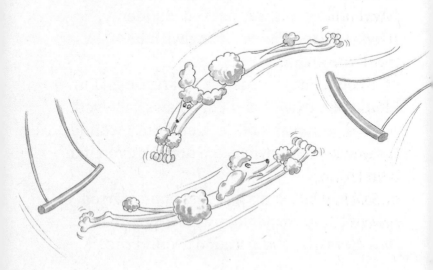

The audience gawked and gasped.

Badger and Pogo Paws rubbed their eyes in wonder, and in her own seat far away, so did Pickle. The movement, speed and colour of the entertainment were like looking through a kaleidoscope.

The ringmaster appeared again and ordered the audience to look up to the high wire above them. "And now, my friends, for the most dangerous of all our acts. Please put your paws together for our very own troupe of *Soaring Angels!*"

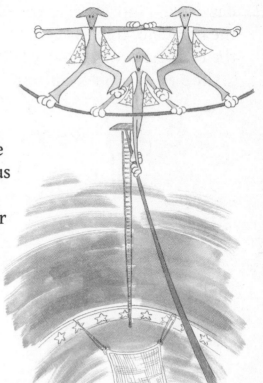

In between acts, the gloopy clowns flabbered and blundered around the ring. Pickle sniggered as she remembered how she and Pogo Paws had transformed themselves into the Tumble Twins earlier in the day.

The performance continued with jugglers, unicyclists, plate-spinners and much much more, until the ringmaster appeared once again, and requested hush in the audience.

"I now bring to you our star attraction of the evening. Never before has such a frightening beast been captured. Nowhere on this living earth, has our next dangerous act, *ever* been found. But tonight, my friends, we bring it to you, straight from its labyrinth in Esterious ...!"

There was a drum roll, and the ringmaster continued: "Let me introduce to you, the only living minotaur in this world; half-big-folk, half-bull. Please put your paws together for *Minty the Mighty*!"

The audience thundered its applause.

The curtain opened to reveal Minty in his cape and chunky boots. He trudged around the ring half-heartedly and roared weakly at the audience. The ringmaster cracked his whip and whispered angrily to the minotaur: "Give it some welly, you ungrateful beast. Terrify them!"

Minty roared more enthusiastically, until the audience held its breath.

"Quick, now's our chance, Pogo Paws," said Badger urgently. "Let's make our way backstage, and I can get my shrinking spell ready for when Minty finishes his routine."

But the invisibility spell was starting to wear off, and as Pogo Paws and Badger sped towards the stage curtain, Pickle spotted the familiar white polka dots of Badger's red neckerchief.

"Aha! There they are. Now's my chance to raise the alarm," thought Pickle.

As Minty took a bow, with the audience whooping and whistling for more, Pickle raced outside to the backstage entrance, to look for the *'please break glass in case of emergency'* box.

The ringmaster cracked his whip, and the guard dogs led Minty offstage and locked him back up in his cage. Crouched behind some haystacks, Badger and Pogo Paws suddenly emerged and stood in front of the minotaur.

"We've got to do this really quickly, Minty," whispered Badger, when the guard dogs had disappeared.

Minty grunted. Badger pointed his ears forward and sparkles of light whirled and whizzed around the cage.

"Now, sit there in the centre, close your eyes and stay very still," instructed Badger, as he uttered the words of the shrinking spell he had practised all day.

"With a sprinkle of Gavaria
And a slapstick wink,
Add an origami shuffle
And a shell bright pink.

Throw in a sunbeam
And a cowpat stink,
Then mix it all up
And make Minty shrink ..."

Badger stood back and hoped that his spell had worked this time. As he did, an almighty siren sounded and all of the circus performers, led by the ringmaster and Pickle, rushed into the backstage area.

"'Chief," ordered Badger at once, "*Show koo ray, show koo ray, please make this chaos go astray. Buzz up a swarm of honeybees, to bring these chasers to their knees.*"

Everything happened at once. Badger's neckerchief flew from his neck, and above them a multitude of bees buzzed. The clowns flapped their arms around their heads in a dither, the jugglers swiped and thrashed, the acrobat cats somersaulted out of the way, the unicyclists floundered, and the ringmaster fled screaming about his precious moustache. Pickle slid away quietly. Badger and Pogo Paws looked back into Minty's cage. The huge beast was nowhere to be seen.

"Over here," squeaked a tiny voice.

Badger and Pogo Paws lay down and looked through the bars of the cage at nose level. There, in front of them, was a really small, toy-sized minotaur.

"It worked!" sighed Badger with relief. "Right, Minty, you can walk through the bars of the cage easily. It's time to introduce you the joys of a higgledy-piggledy tower of toast back at mine. I think we all deserve a treat."

"Where did Pickle go?" asked Pogo Paws looking around.

"I don't know, but I suspect *she* sounded the alarm. She clearly doesn't want you to go, Pogo Paws," said Badger firmly.

Badger picked up Minty in his paw, and headed back to his garden, followed by a dejected Pogo Paws.

Back at the circus, and lost in the darkness, Pickle had found her way into the Hall of Crazy Mirrors.

Chapter Eight

Pickle shivered and thought, *This Hall of Crazy Mirrors is scary.* Everywhere she turned, she could see more Pickles in different stretched shapes and squished sizes. The hall smelt musty and mouldy. Whenever she stood in front of one of the mirrors, it lit up and shrieked at her.

"Mirror, mirror on the wall, I can make you big and tall," wittered the voice from the distorted reflection before her. She moved on to the next looking glass.

"*Here's looking at you, kid,*" came the voice from behind the wobbly image of herself.

The next curved mirror made her look bendy and whispered, "*Right back at you*".

The next one yelled out, "*Scaramouche!*" and multiplied her face in odd directions.

At last, she reached the final mirror. "*Here we can see ourselves as others see us,*" screeched the menacing voice from behind.

Pickle was baffled. In it, she looked bitter and

84

unkind. Her fur was matted and dirty, and her new collar was threadbare. She peered closer. Her reflected smile was crooked, and she really didn't seem like a very nice person to know.

"*Here we can see ourselves as others see us,*" repeated the voice. "*Change your ways now, Pickle. Stop being so selfish or you will lose Pogo Paws anyway.*"

Pickle poked and prodded the mirror. "What *are* you talking about?" she demanded.

Just then, the Hall of Crazy Mirrors was overrun with flip-flopping clowns. They swept up Pickle and bundled her off.

Back in Badger's garden, the Mystical Mutt, Pogo Paws and the tiny minotaur were tucking into some hot-buttered toast, and discussing the next day's trip to the Crystal

Cave, and the plan for the Enchanting Exchange.

"Just crumbs for you, Minty. You're far too small to manage a full slice of your own," smiled Badger, as butter dribbled down his chin. He winked at Pogo Paws and said, "Which means more for us, of course!"

Suddenly, Badger saw a pair of huge flipper shoes pass the fence, and something was thrown over onto the grass: a large, white envelope addressed to Badger.

"I usually get my post via p-mail. What can this be?" said Badger, opening the letter. There in cut-out newspaper letters was a shoddy ransom note that said: *"HAND OVER THE MINOTAUR BY SUNRISE TOMORROW, AND YOU WILL GET PICKLE BACK!"*

"Oh no, Pogo Paws. The circus has kidnapped Pickle. They'll return her safely, if we hand over Minty. But it's nearly midnight. We've only got until tomorrow morning to do the Enchanting Exchange"

Minty sighed miserably. "Maybe it's just

not meant to be. Maybe I'm destined to spend my life in the circus, and I'll never return home."

Pogo Paws whined. "I can't leave Pickle at the circus. She'll end up acrobatting, and her balancing skills are rubbish! Maybe I need to stay here and look after her."

Badger looked from Minty to Pogo Paws, and from Pogo Paws to Minty and smiled: "Turn those frowns upside-down, you two. Maybe there's a way this can work out for everyone. I just haven't figured out how to make that happen yet. But give me time ... and I will."

"But we don't have any time!" shouted Pogo Paws and Minty together.

Backstage at the circus, Pickle was not happy. She was in the one place she really didn't want to be. Added to which, she was blindfolded and tied up. She really missed bickering with Pogo Paws. She'd even grown fond of Badger lately. She wanted to be back home on the lane.

"Let's see how much your precious pals really love you," sneered one of the clowns, squirting water in her face. "We've sent your beloved Pogo Paws and Badger a ransom note. If they don't hand over Minty the Mighty before sunrise, we're sending you to the wire ... the high wire!" The clown cackled and clattered off.

Oh no, thought Pickle, *this is all my fault. I wonder if Badger and Pogo Paws will come to my rescue? I wonder if they'll even care?* She closed her eyes to try and sleep, but she could not shut out the nasty image of herself in the last of the mirrors. *If that's how I appear to others, then I really will be stuck here forever...*

Back at Badger's, the two dogs and the little minotaur were in a huddle discussing a plan.

"I'm still shrunk," said Minty helpfully. "So, *I* can sneak in and get Pickle."

"*I'll* take on all of them," offered Pogo Paws bravely. "Nobody does this to my pal Pickle."

"Yes, but they'll be expecting us," said Badger. "And let's remember that the ringmaster has a whip and couple of pretty fierce guard dogs. No, we need to hoodwink the circus into believing Pickle has escaped herself. Now, let me think."

They all sat quietly for a few moment, and then Badger leapt up and danced around.

"I've got it! Now, Pogo Paws, do you still have those clown disguises you used earlier?"

"Yes," Pogo Paws answered warily. "They're in the trunk in your shed. We never had a chance to return them."

"Good! Right, now listen carefully. Here's the plan ..." whispered Badger.

Chapter Nine

In the early hours of the next morning, before the sun had risen, Badger awoke, all too aware that an important day lay ahead. He shook Pogo Paws gently, and nudged Minty.

Pickle, too, awoke in her makeshift bed of a haystack, and stretched as best she could. Her paws were sore from the twine tied around them. Her blindfold had shifted slightly and she could see that daylight was dawning.

They never came for me after all. So it's the circus life for me, from now on, she thought sadly. *That mirror was so true when it told me to change my ways or I'd lose Pogo Paws anyway.*

But not too far away, a spiky haired, big-footed clown was already making its way into the enclosure where Pickle was imprisoned.

As the blindfold was untied from Pickle's head and the twine around her paws came undone, she rubbed the darkness away from her eyes. There, in front of her, was Pogo Paws, smiling.

"You didn't really believe I could leave you here, did you? You're rubbish at balancing. You'd never survive in a circus,"

said Pogo Paws affectionately.

Pickle jumped up and hugged him tightly.

"I am so very, very sorry, Pogo Paws. I was being selfish. I just didn't want you to leave. But I understand now ... that if I care at all for you, then I have to let you go."

Pogo Paws was surprised. He had never seen such warmth before from Pickle. He patted her paw gently.

"I know," he said. "I *will* miss you, but I'll *never* forget you. Surely the memories we share mean something? Just because we can't see each other doesn't mean we won't always be in each other's hearts."

"So, you're still going then?" asked Pickle haughtily.

"I am. Although, if you really don't want me to go, then I won't. Or you could always come with me?" suggested Pogo Paws hopefully

Pickle gulped, remembering the mirror's wise words, and said: "No, you must go. You've talked about nothing else since we first met all those years ago. And *my* home is on the lane. You said it yourself: I'd *never* survive in a circus."

"Thank you, Pickle. Okay then, we have to get you away from here until the solar eclipse, and then I need you to help me in the circus ring."

"Stop right there! I have *no* idea what you are talking about. What or who is *Silvery Lips*? Is that another one of the circus acts?

Pogo Paws smirked and explained. "A *solar eclipse* — not *silvery lips*, Pickle — is when the sun is blacked out by the moon. During a total eclipse, all we will see is a ring of light. Then, and only then, can the Enchanting Exchange take place"

"Epic! And what? There's one of these things happening today?" said Pickle awestruck.

"Yes, very soon. And that's why I really need your help. Now come on, we need to hide. Follow me," said Pogo Paws.

They made their way to the benched seating, and crawled underneath before the circus realised their hostage had escaped.

Soon, the circus began to wake up, and discovered that Pickle had vanished. The siren sounded and woozy clowns and slumbering acrobatic cats emerged from their tents. The ringmaster rounded up his search parties and sent them off towards the lane, and a certain Mystical Mutt's garden.

But Badger was already high in the skies heading for Nippy Nimbus, the gatekeeper to the Enchanted Forest, with a gradually growing minotaur.

"Uh oh!" said Badger. "I think my shrinking spell is starting to wear off. I hope we make it to the Crystal Cave before it does, because I don't think the Wim-Wim can take your weight."

The Wim-Wim struggled to climb higher and Badger looked around frantically for anything he could throw overboard to lighten the load. He spotted some heavy spell books on the floor, and chucked them quickly over the side. At once, the Wim-Wim soared higher and higher, and soon Badger spotted Nippy Nimbus, the grumpiest cloud in the world, nearby.

Nippy moaned as the Wim-Wim approached to land. "You again, Badger?"

"Afraid so, Nippy. Now, about this password malarkey, do we really still need to go through all that? Or can you just let me pass? I'm in a dreadful rush."

"Oh come on, Badger. Where would the fun be if I did that? Give me your best shot, go on," said Nippy, daring him to guess the password correctly.

Badger scratched the white tuft on the top of his head and said: "How about *Send in the clowns*?"

"Nice try, but er ... wrong! Try again!" commanded Nippy.

"Okay, let's try *Tears of a clown*?" said Badger, a little impatiently.

"Close, but er ... no. One last try."

"Right, this has got to be it because it's exactly how I feel. *Stuck in the middle with you.*"

"Yes, you did it! Make your way down the usual way," ordered Nippy.

Badger opened the trapdoor and looked

down. "Come on, Minty," he beckoned.
But the minotaur was struggling to get out
of the Wim-Wim, and was wedged snugly
inside.

"I think the spell has completely worn off
now, Badger. I seem to be full size again,"
said the minotaur, who had blushed as
crimson as its cape.

"Okay, hang on! I think I can get you out.
Deep breaths," said Badger hopefully.

Badger prised and squeezed, and pinched
and squashed, until Minty's cumbersome
body popped out of the Wim-Wim.

"Phew!" panted Badger. "That was jam-
packed."

But as Minty stepped further onto Nippy
Nimbus, the cloud groaned and fell a good
bit lower.

"Oh no!" Nippy grimaced. "Look what
you've made me do! I'm now officially
low cloud, which means I'll have to rain.
I wasn't due to rain for days yet. Now,
I'll have to write a report for the Drizzle
Doctors ..."

"Quick, let's get out of here," said Badger as they both flung themselves through the trapdoor, to land with a heavy thud in the Enchanted Forest. Luckily, the now full-size minotaur landed first, with Badger falling on top, narrowly missing Minty's horns.

"Okay, where now?" asked Minty, shaking his massive head and dusting down his cape.

"Now, we wait for our friend Baby Unicorn," said Badger quietly.

"What's that over there?" asked Minty, spying a rustling bush ahead.

"That's the Hurry Hedge. Why don't you peek your head through and take a look?" suggested Badger.

Minty moved towards the greenery and poked his head cautiously into the bush. On the other side, everything was speeded up. Bees buzzed at 100 miles an hour, birds zipped through the air with a whoosh, and plants grew visibly bigger in front of the minotaur's eyes.

"Whoah!" said Minty, pulling his head out to face Badger again "That's making my head spin. What's it all about?"

"That, my friend, is Sprummer," said Badger wisely.

"Sprummer?" asked Minty "I've never heard of it."

"That's because it's the fifth season, and only exists here in the Enchanted Forest. Back in the lane, we have Spring, Summer, Autumn and Winter. Here, Sprummer is between Spring and Summer, and it's where everything moves as fast as we sometimes wish it would. It's a lesson for us and the Big Folk below, to take our time to enjoy the present."

"I don't understand," said Minty, scrunching his eyes.

"Well, you're really keen to get back home, but are you absolutely sure that's what you really want? It's all happened pretty quickly since we met. There's no going back from this, once the Exchange is complete. That's it, it cannot be reversed.

Sometimes, we move so fast, we don't take time to think about things. So you have to be truly sure that you want to return."

Minty was very quiet, then said: "Yes, I'm sure. There's only one place I call home, and that's my labyrinth, so let's go! Where's your pal?"

Just then, Baby Unicorn appeared around the side of the Hurry Hedge.

"Hello, Badger, and you must be Minty," said the unicorn.

"Wow!" said Minty, a little smitten with the beautiful white creature. "Your one horn is massively more impressive than mine, and I've got *two* of them."

Baby Unicorn bowed and thanked the minotaur graciously. "I believe I can help you. Follow me." The unicorn swished its tail and led the way to the Crystal Cave.

Back at the circus, the site was deserted but for Pogo Paws and Pickle. Everyone else was off on a Pickle-hunt. The two dogs lifted the canvas and peeked out from under the candy striped Big Top tent. The sun was getting higher in the sky; the eclipse could not be far away now.

Pogo Paws changed out of his Tumble Twin clown outfit and took his position in the centre of the circus ring. He sniffed the air around him; it smelled of sawdust and greasepaint.

He smiled. All he had to do now was wait.

As instructed by Pogo Paws, Pickle stood on the platform above, where the lighting rigs hung, ready to shine the spotlight onto her beloved pal, when the all-important moment arrived.

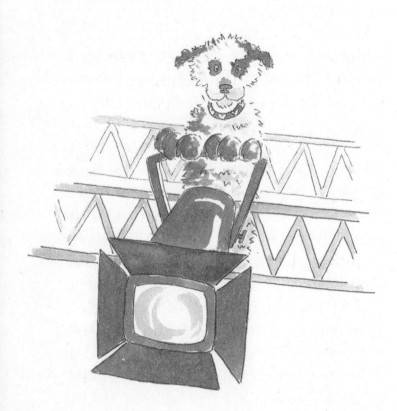

Chapter Ten

Badger had never been this far into the Crystal Cave before. He and Minty followed Baby Unicorn as they ventured deeper and deeper in. The minotaur was wide-eyed as they walked along paths of pure crystal, past walls of glitter.

Finally, when it looked like they could go no further, Baby Unicorn's horn began to glow brightly. He touched the tip of his horn on a pulsating stalagmite, and suddenly, an opening appeared in the cave wall. The unicorn nodded for them to go through. On the other side of the rock, was a small circle of ancient standing stones. At the very centre was a tiny shaft of daylight. Badger looked upwards and saw an opening to the sky.

"Okay," said Baby Unicorn "This is it. Here we are. Now, Minty, step into the circle and stand perfectly still in that patch of light … and wait."

"Wait? Wait for what?" asked Minty timidly.

"For the total solar eclipse," said Badger. "Goodness, this is really happening. You did mean it. I can actually go home this time, after all," said Minty smiling.

"Yes, if I can get the spell right, Minty. I hope I don't let you down." Badger turned to Baby Unicorn and asked: "So, even here in the Enchanted Forest, do the planets move the same as in the lane?"

"As above, as below," said the unicorn wisely. "It may seem like time stands still when you visit me here, Badger, but we're all still under the same sky."

"But not through the Hurry Hedge?" asked Badger.

"Now, *that's* a trick of the light," said Baby Unicorn.

Badger scratched his chin and practised the spell over and over in his head. The patch of light was continuing to get smaller.

In the circus ring, the Big Top's apex was getting darker. Pickle's paws trembled, poised to switch on the powerful spotlight.

"This has got to be precise," shouted Pogo Paws. "Not a moment too soon, or a moment too late."

"I'm ready, Pogo Paws," yelled Pickle, hoping she could synchronise the Exchange perfectly for her friend, although there was also a little bit of her, hoping that it *wouldn't* work.

In the Crystal Cave, they were almost in darkness.

Seconds later, in the circus tent, it was a complete black-out.

"Now!" cried Pogo Paws to Pickle as she hit the switch.

At exactly the same moment, in the Crystal Cave, Badger uttered the sacred words of the spell; the most powerful magic, he had *ever* done:

"With pebbles from Pluto
And red dust from Mars,
Let the Enchanting Exchange
Begin with the stars...
With a solar eclipse
And a charmed bewitch,
Shine the light forth
On this magical switch ..."

A beam of beautiful golden light shot down from the very top of the Crystal Cave to the spot where Minty stood in the stone circle, dazzling both Badger and Baby Unicorn.

In the circus tent, the brilliant spotlight shone down so brightly that Pickle shielded her eyes and had to look away.

Then all was very, very quiet.

Pickle looked down. The spotlight had gone ... and so had her friend.

All that remained was an empty, dusty circus ring.

In the Crystal Cave, the tiny patch of sunlight had returned, but Minty had disappeared.

Baby Unicorn and Badger were alone in the cave.

"A badgical-magical job well done?" whispered Badger nervously.

"Indeed!" said the unicorn. "You should be very proud of yourself, Badger. Not everyone can command a spell as powerful as that. Now, come with me. I'd like to show you something that will set your mind at ease."

Badger followed Baby Unicorn to the usual spot in the cave, which lit up into a screen. The unicorn pointed his horn at the wall, and Badger saw Minty bumbling about his labyrinth, as if he was watching it all on TV. Hanging over the entrance to the maze, was a sign with the words *Home Sweet Home*.

"Happy now?" asked the unicorn gently. "The minotaur is now exactly where he wanted to be. You did well, Badger. And now for something else ..."

The unicorn pointed its horn again at the screen like it was switching channels. There, in front of them both was a picture of Pogo Paws meeting his family inside a big circus tent. But it wasn't the circus from the lane. This was Pogo Paws' circus from his childhood, and he was smiling from ear to ear.

"He made it too then," said Badger thoughtfully. "Pickle must have helped him in the end. Maybe she really *did* care for him after all?"

"When you love somebody, Badger, sometimes the hardest thing is to set them free. But Pickle will be fine. She's got you and she's got friends."

"Hmmm!" Badger wasn't so sure. "She's got me anyway. She might have to work on her manners a little to get some pals."

"Anyway, you must go now, my friend," said the unicorn. "Haven't you got a fence to fix?"

Badger looked baffled.

"That minotaur-sized hole?"

"Aha, of course!" said Badger chuckling, "Thank you for all your help. See you next time"

Badger boarded his Wim-Wim and headed for home.

Chapter Eleven

Pickle was already in Badger's garden, awaiting his arrival home. She was sheltering inside the shed, as another massive thunderstorm rumbled around her. The air crackled and sparked with lightning, and big drops of rain were battering the roof of the shed.

Suddenly, the door of the shed swung open and Pickle looked up to see Badger drenched and shivering.

"Come in, quickly, before you get any wetter," she said, ushering him inside.

"It doesn't seem so long ago that we were all sitting in here together, watching the thunderstorm the day the circus came to town," said Badger.

"Yes, and I know Pogo Paws was a scaredy cat about it, although he pretended he wasn't," said Pickle fondly.

"I see you fixed the fence," said Badger.

"Fence? What do you mean? I haven't touched it."

"Oh!" said Badger, wondering if the minotaur-shaped hole in it had melded magically when Minty had gone back home.

"I *am* sad without him," said Pickle forlornly. "I miss him *so* much."

"I know, Pickle. I miss him too. But we have to believe that he is much happier now. He's where he wanted to be, and I saw a glimpse of it in the Crystal Cave. He's having a great time, and he's with all of his own family now."

Pickle sighed.

"And for once," continued the Mystical Mutt, "doesn't it make you feel good to know that you did the right thing?"

"Perhaps," said Pickle pitifully.

"Okay enough of this gloomity glumdrum. I'm going to try one of my cheery up spells. Are you sitting comfortably?"

"Oh, Badger, how is that you're usually rubbish at spells, yet you managed to make the Enchanting Exchange one work?"

"I'm not quite sure myself, Pickle. Maybe because it was meant to be? Now, let's try this one:

Crunchy munchy chewy chops,
Buddy bites and bones,
Lollipops and candy bars
And ice-cream cones.
Tasty treats and snoozes
Will help through thick and thin,
So cheery up your sorrow
And fix it with a grin."

Badger sat back feeling quite pleased with himself. "There, now how does that feel?"

"I'm still a bit sad, but thanks for trying," sighed Pickle, touching her lilac collar.

"Okay. How about some toast? That might help," said Badger hopefully.

But even the lure of some hot-buttered toast couldn't seem to lift Pickle's spirits.

"I'm not very hungry, Badger. I think I'll go for a walk instead," she said, as she slipped through the crack in the fence.

Badger stayed in his shed for a while, trying to think of something that would make Pickle feel less sad.

Pickle padded towards the site of the circus.

Everything had gone. The storm had passed but the grass was still muddy.

All she could see were some torn posters flapping in the breeze, wagon tracks and a few broken tent pegs. As she turned to go back to the lane, she caught the whiff of a recent p-mail.

It was from Pogo Paws. He must have sent it earlier in the morning, before the Enchanting Exchange.

She smiled as she read his words:
Dearest Pickle,
I've only gone next door. Speak to me as Pogo
Paws and nag me like you always did. Think
of good times on the lane, and the fun we had.
These memories will always remain in our
hearts. I'm just around the corner, and all is

119

well. I hope you don't mind me sending you a p-mail from time to time.
Your friend
Pogo Paws

As Pickle made her way home, she wagged her tail for the first time that day.

Chapter Twelve

As a brand new day dawned, Pickle was now on her own, mooching down the lane, idly kicking tin cans and bin lids. She sniffed the fresh breeze. The storm had finally passed. As she reached the crack in the fence of Badger's garden, she heard a huge commotion coming from his shed.

Goodness, she thought. *What on earth is the Mystical Mutt up to now?*

She scrambled into the garden and rapped sharply on the shed door.

"Er ... Badger? Hello? Is everything okay?" she asked.

The door burst open. Hundreds of wellie boots and multi-coloured balls flew out, whizzing and whirling around the garden, knocking Pickle to the ground.

"Sorry about that," said Badger apologetically. "I was practising my latest wellie boots and balls trick. Only it didn't quite work."

Pickle looked at Badger bewilderedly. Badger looked at Pickle sheepishly.

They both burst out laughing.

"Well, at least I've made you laugh," giggled Badger.

"Pogo Paws would have loved that;" said Pickle brushing herself down, "all that bouncing around. I really miss him, Badger."

"I know," said Badger gently.

"I got what I always wanted. I'm now sole leader of the gang, except I haven't got a gang anymore. Everyone's left, and I don't fancy bossing myself about much," she said forlornly. "In fact, I haven't got anyone now. Pogo Paws was my best and only friend."

Badger gave her a cuddle.

"Although," she added, sniffing, "I picked up a p-mail from him yesterday. He must have sent it before he left. And it was like I could hear his voice again."

"Our loved ones never truly leave us, Pickle," said Badger kindly. "And I'm sure you'll get more p-mails from him."

Then he rubbed his white tuft on the top of his head and thought for a moment.

"Maybe you can use your position as gang leader for good, for a change?" suggested Badger.

"Good? I don't think I've ever been good. The mirror in the circus showed me that," said Pickle.

"Being leader isn't about being bossy and horrible. You could make a difference to lots of cats and dogs on the lane, if you used your position as leader to give a helping hand now and again," said Badger.

"Oh, I don't really know" said Pickle frowning. "That's not the way I usually do things."

"Yes, but everything has changed, Pickle. Nothing is *usual* anymore. How about I help you to round up some of the old gang, and set up a new bunch; a good crew?" offered Badger.

"I don't think any of them will talk to me ever again. I was so nasty," said Pickle.

"I wouldn't be so sure. I got a p-mail from Dodgy Dave and Cheryl recently. They're due back from their tour of Blackpool soon. Hamish and Top Dog are still here, up the lane, and Snif and Timmy are doing a fine job at PLOPP, the drop-in centre round the corner. Even my cousin, The Earl of Doodlepoppington, is flying in from Persia to pay me a visit shortly. It'll be just like old times."

"I'll still be the one that no one wants to talk to," said Pickle glumly.

"Not if you show them you've changed your ways. Believe me, we dogs and cats don't hold grudges for long." Badger scratched his chin and added, "Well, actually, maybe *cats* do ..."

"Timmy isn't like a normal cat though," laughed Pickle.

"Too true, too true," Badger chuckled. "So, it's up to you, Pickle, but you know I'll help however I can."

"As far as getting the old gang back together ... it won't be the same without Pogo Paws, will it?" said Pickle.

"It won't be quite the same, no. But a different kind of same perhaps?" suggested Badger wisely.

"Okay," said Pickle, a little befuddled. "Thank you. I'll think about it."

"Marvellous! Now, would you like some toast? It's been quite an exhausting badgical-magical time recently," said Badger sighing.

"Actually, I've got to go and chase some pesky birds off my patch. See you later, your Mystical Muttness!"

Pickle saluted Badger, and slipped through the crack in the fence.

Badger shook himself and mulled over the idea of trying to bring Pogo Paws back for a gang reunion. He shuddered slightly at the thought; not of Pogo Paws alone, but of *all* the gang! Individually was one thing ... but together? Top Dog, Dodgy Dave, Snif, Lennie, Pickle and Pogo Paws?

And as he lay his head down on the slightly damp grass, he wondered just how chaotic his next adventure would be.

ALSO PUBLISHED BY THE LUNICORN PRESS

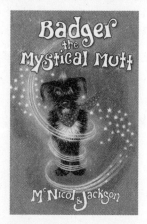

Badger the Mystical Mutt
ISBN: 978-0-9569640-0-7

**Badger the Mystical Mutt
and the Barking Boogie**
ISBN: 978-0-9560640-1-4

**Badger the Mystical Mutt
and the Crumpled Capers**
ISBN: 978-0-9569640-2-1

**Badger the Mystical Mutt
and the Daydream Drivers**
ISBN: 978-0-9569640-4-5

www.badgerthemysticalmutt.com